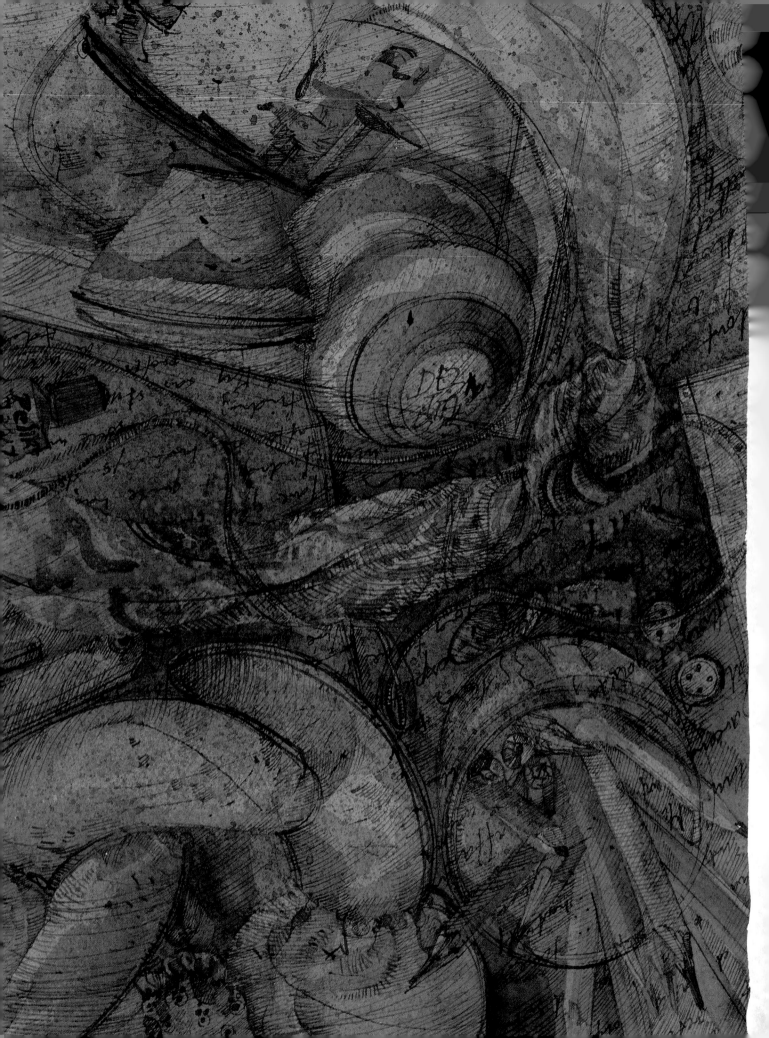

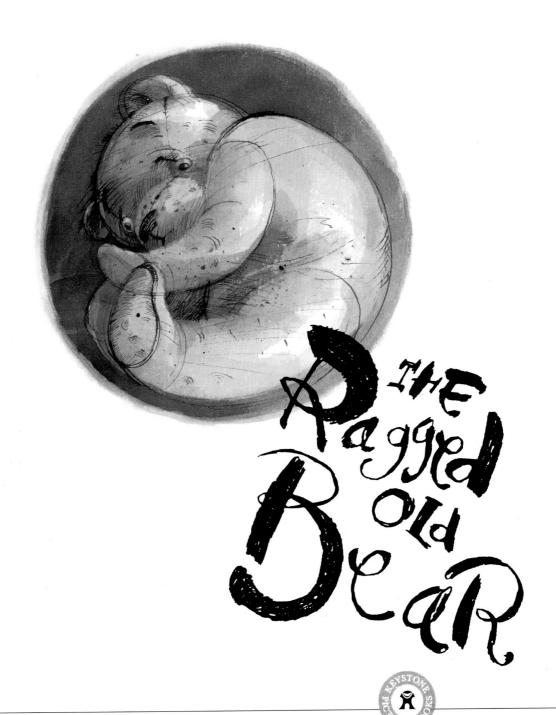

THE Ragged old BEAR

KEYSTONE PICTURE BOOKS

TEXT LEONE PEGUERO

ILLUSTRATION DONNA GYNELL

Special thanks to Zareena and 'Big Ted'
and to Llian for her patience   D.G.

Produced by Martin International Pty Ltd
[A.C.N. 008 210 642] South Australia
Published in association with Era Publications,
220 Grange Road, Flinders Park,
South Australia 5025

Text © Leone Peguero, 1992
Illustrations © Donna Gynell, 1992
Design by Donna Gynell
Printed in Hong Kong
First Published 1992

**National Library of Australia
Cataloguing-in-Publication Data:**

Peguero, Leone.
         The ragged old bear.

     ISBN 1 86374 020 1.

     1. Teddy Bears - Juvenile fiction.
     I. Gynell, Donna, 1960-   . II. Title.

A823.3

Available in:

Australia from Era Publications,
220 Grange Road, Flinders Park,
South Australia 5025

Canada from Vanwell Publishing Ltd,
1 Northrup Cresc., PO Box 2131,
Stn B, St Catharines, ONT L2M 6P5

New Zealand from Wheelers Bookclub,
PO Box 35-586,
Browns Bay, Auckland 10

Singapore, Malaysia & Brunei from
Publishers Marketing Services Pte Ltd,
10-C Jalan Ampas,
#07-01 Ho Seng Lee Flatted Warehouse,
Singapore 1232

United Kingdom from Ragged Bears,
Ragged Appleshaw,
Andover, Hampshire SP11 9HX

United States of America from
AUSTRALIAN PRESS™, c/- Ed-Tex,
15235 Brand Blvd., #A107,
Mission Hills CA 91345

Josi wanted to take her friends
with her when she went out.

But furry, white rabbits get dirty
so easily. Computer toys break if
you drop them. And china dolls,
like baby birds, can be hurt if
you hold them too much.

So all Josi's friends had
to stay at home.

When she visited Granny,
Josi didn't mind so much
leaving her friends behind.
Granny had a spare room full
of old toys, books and games.
It was here one day that Josi
discovered a ragged, old bear
in a wooden box.

Josi loved him at once.

"Oh, that old thing," said Granny.
"I haven't seen him for years."

"You wouldn't want such
a ragged, old toy,"
said Josi's mother.

But Josi did want him.
He wasn't delicate
and no one cared if
he got dirty or damaged.
At least no one cared but Josi.

Bear's new life began in
a bucket of soap suds.

"Will the suds hurt him?"
asked Josi anxiously.

"That depends on what he's
made of," said Josi's mother.

Bear must have been made
of sturdy stuff, because
he survived just as he had
for many years.

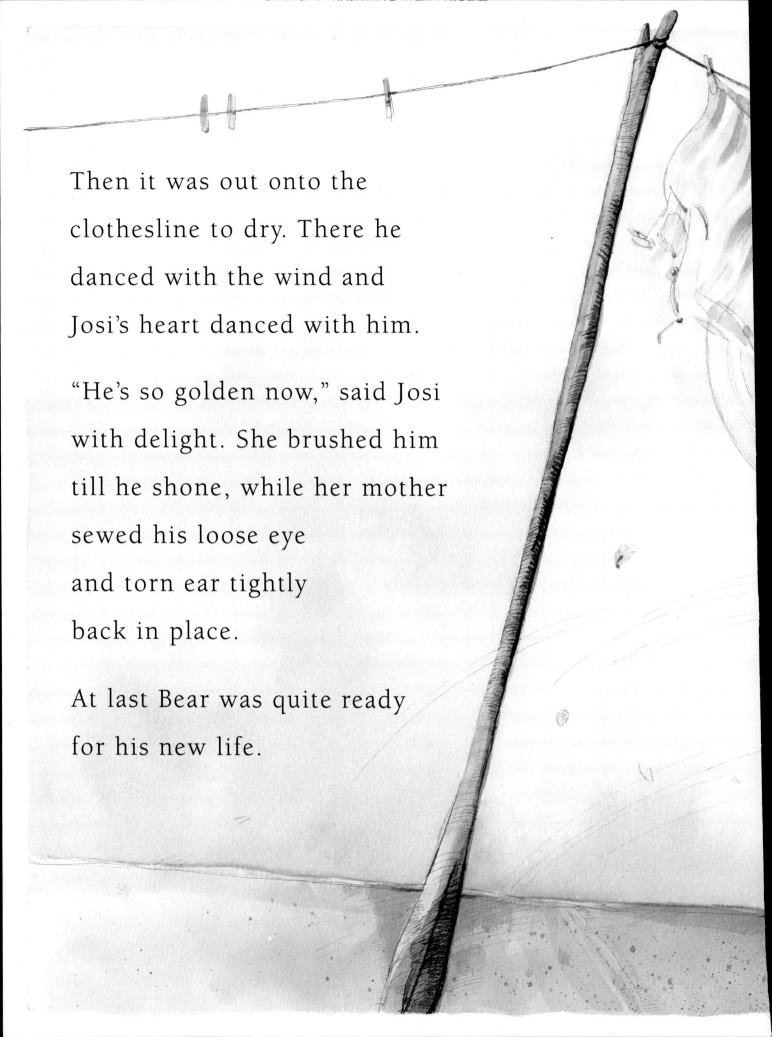

Then it was out onto the
clothesline to dry. There he
danced with the wind and
Josi's heart danced with him.

"He's so golden now," said Josi
with delight. She brushed him
till he shone, while her mother
sewed his loose eye
and torn ear tightly
back in place.

At last Bear was quite ready
for his new life.

Since he wasn't new or delicate,
Josi was able to take Bear almost
anywhere. There were so many
exciting things for them to do.
He and Josi had much to talk
about and Bear was a very
careful listener.

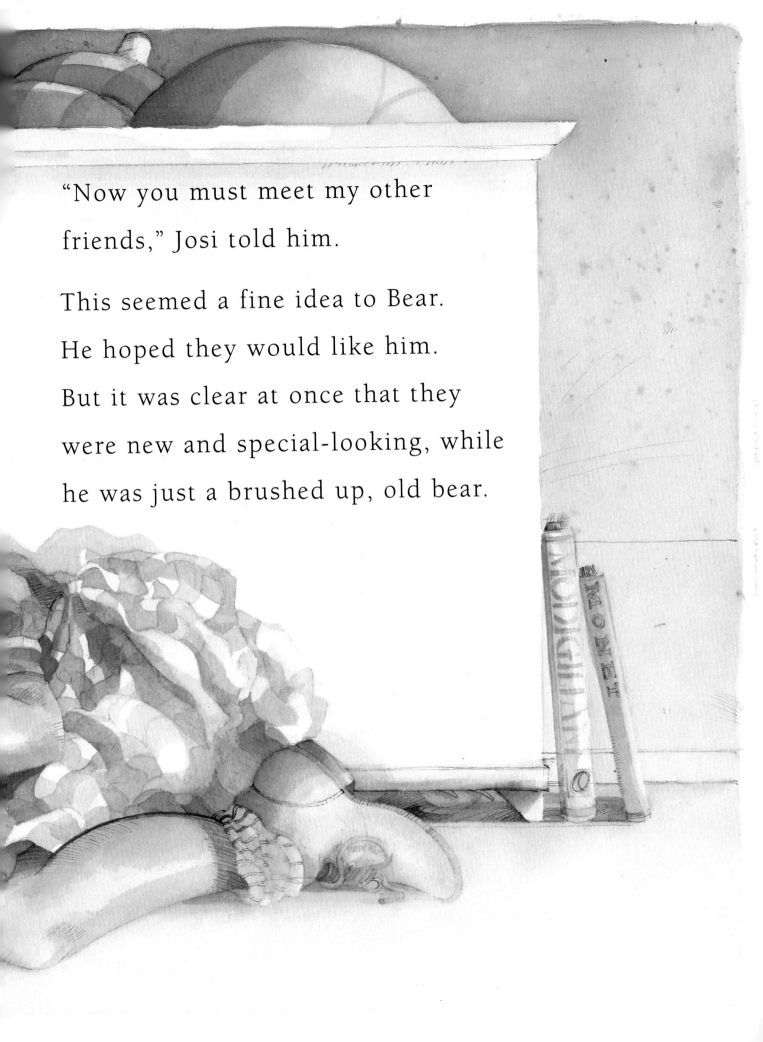

"Now you must meet my other friends," Josi told him.

This seemed a fine idea to Bear. He hoped they would like him. But it was clear at once that they were new and special-looking, while he was just a brushed up, old bear.

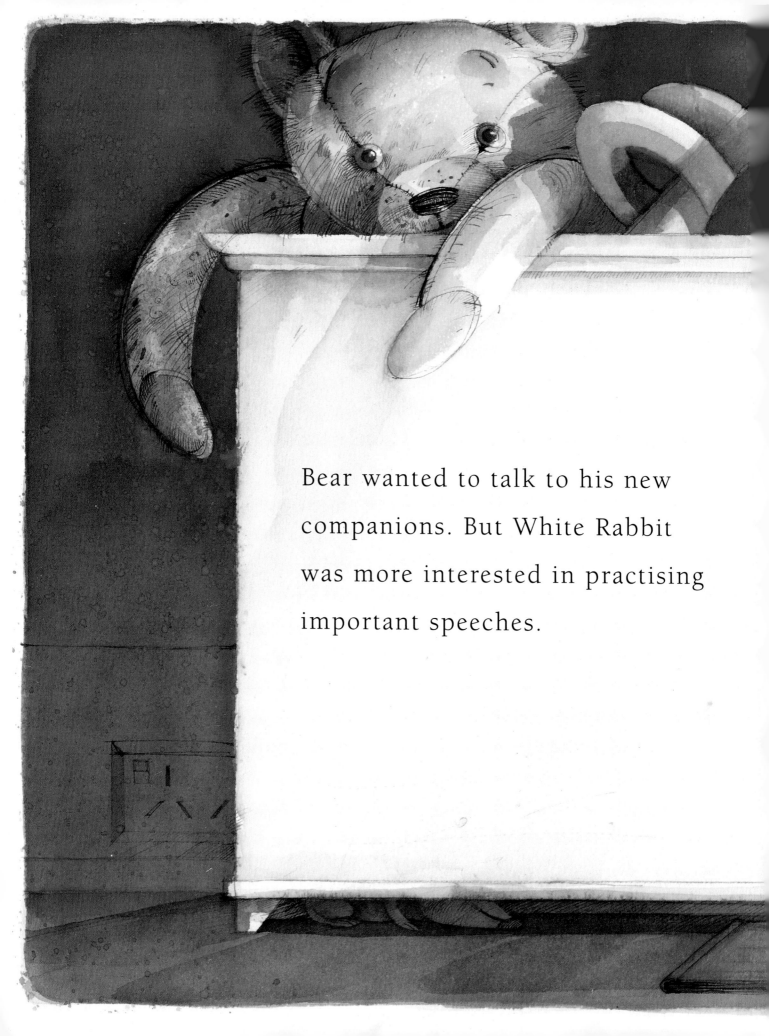

Bear wanted to talk to his new
companions. But White Rabbit
was more interested in practising
important speeches.

Robo-teach was always murmuring
to herself as if she were considering
something deep and important.

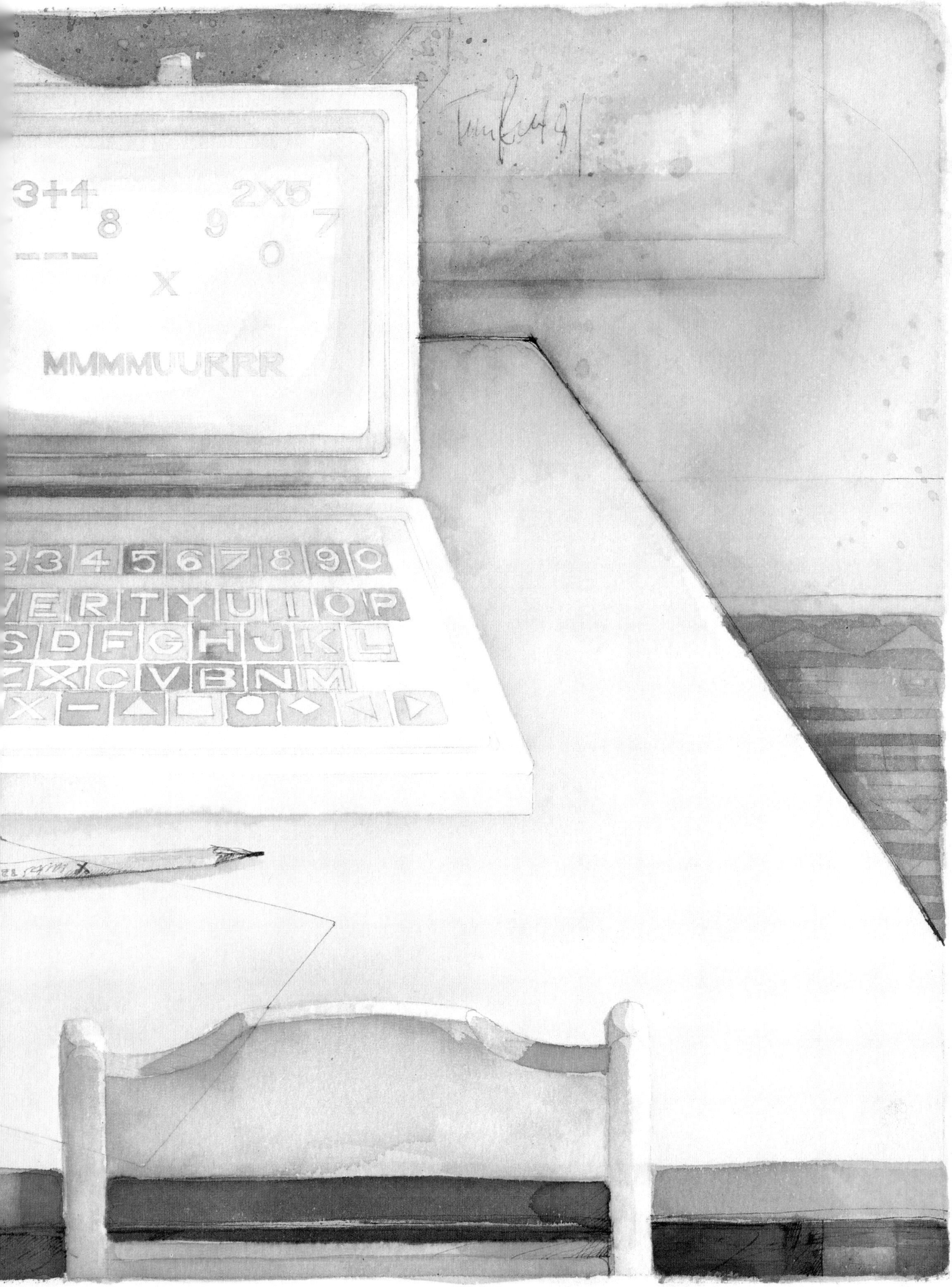
3+4
2X5
8
9
7
0
X
MMMMUURRR

And Angelica spent so much time
practising her dancing,
that there was no time for conversation.
So, when Josi was not around,
Bear sat on his own.

Bear knew that none of this
should matter, but sometimes
he wished that he looked as
dignified as White Rabbit;

or that he could be
as clever as Robo-teach
and solve problems
as easily as she could;

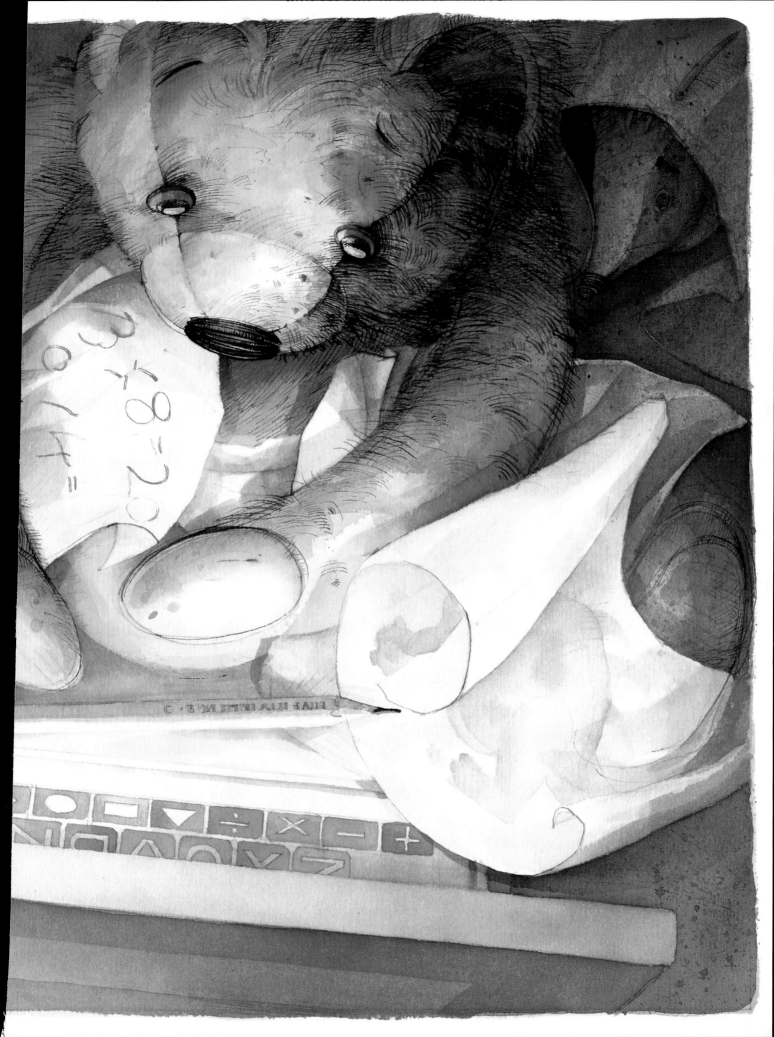

or that he was as graceful

as Angelica. But he wasn't.

He was just a ragged, old bear.

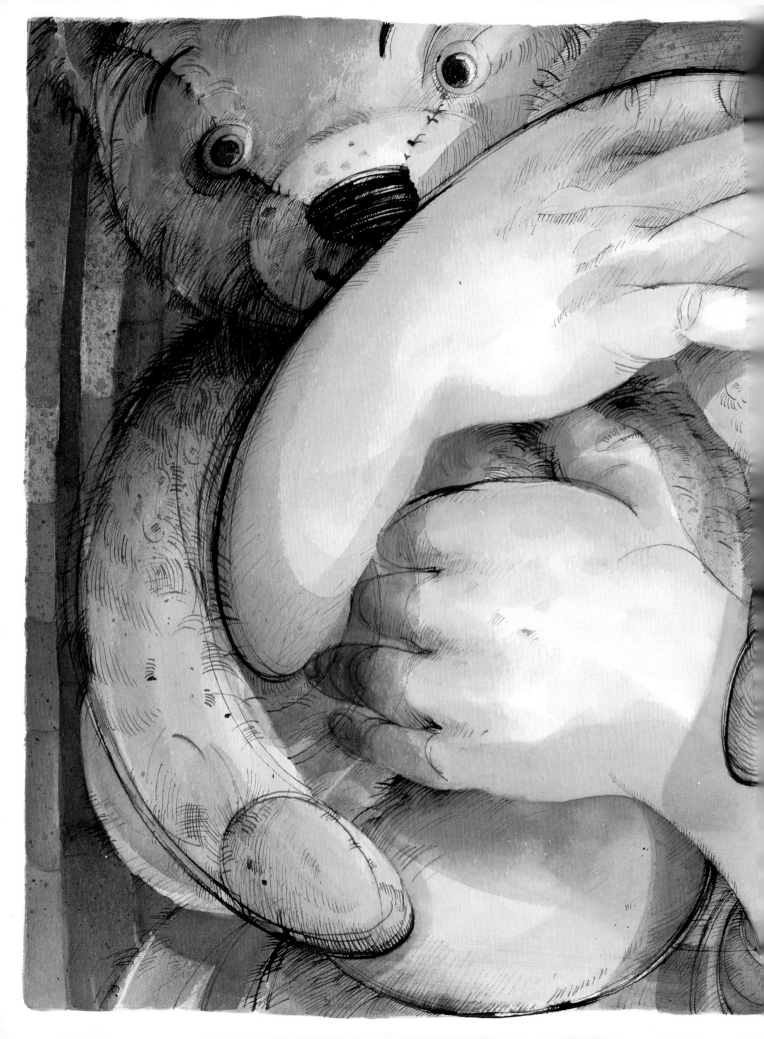

Then Bear remembered
all that his new life
had become; how he
had been rescued
from the wooden box,
cared for and taken
all kinds of places.

Most of all, he remembered
how Josi loved him.
That was something
to celebrate.

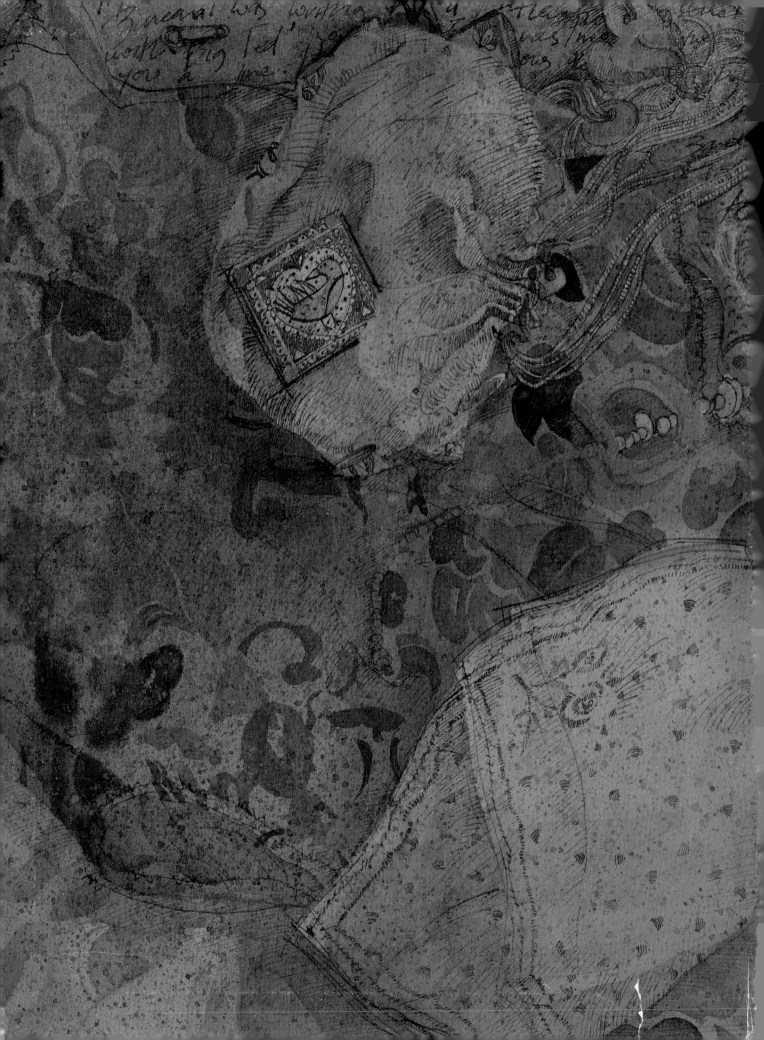